DOCTOR·WHO

DECIDE YOUR DESTINY

BBC CHILDREN'S BOOKS
Published by the Penguin Group
Penguin Books Ltd, 80 Strand, London, WC2R 0RL, England
Penguin Group (USA) Inc., 375 Hudson Street, New York, New York 10014, USA
Penguin Books (Australia) Ltd, 250 Camberwell Road, Camberwell, Victoria 3124,
Australia
(A division of Pearson Australia Group Pty Ltd)
Canada, India, New Zealand, South Africa
Published by BBC Children's Books, 2007
This edition produced for The Book People Ltd, Hall Wood Avenue, Haydock, St Helens. WA11 9UL.
Text and design © Children's Character Books, 2007
Written by Trevor Baxendale
10 9 8 7 6 5 4 3 2 1
ISBN-13: 978-1-85613-158-2
ISBN-10: 1-85613-158-0
Printed in Great Britain by Clays Ltd, St Ives plc

DOCTOR·WHO

DECIDE YOUR DESTINY

The Dragon King

by Trevor Baxendale

The Dragon King

1 | It's been raining all weekend. You're stuck in the house doing boring homework. Your mind's a blank and all you can do is watch the rain pouring down the window.

It's hard to tell through the rain, but a large blue box seems to have appeared on the pavement outside your house. It wasn't there a minute ago.

Ditching the homework, you run outside to investigate.

It's a police box — at least, that's what it says on the sign above the doors. You try to peer in through the little frosted glass windows at the top of the doors but you can't quite reach them. But as you touch the doors, they swing open.

Inside is an impossibly large room with a high domed roof and a complicated, central control console. Struggling with the controls is a tall, skinny-looking man with dark spiky hair and lively eyes.

He sees you — just as a loud, strange groaning sound fills the chamber.

'What?' he exclaims, his eyes wide with sudden concern. 'Close the doors! We're dematerialising!'

If you close the doors, go to 27. If you don't manage it, go to 42.

2 | You scramble quickly through the hole in the tent.

Outside it's chaos. The Elanden are running scared. A squad of golden aliens in black spacesuits, bristling with weapons, are striding through the camp. They are clearly more advanced than the natives and quickly start subduing them with energy weapons. The fizz and zap of disruptor beams fill the air and many villagers fall.

There's little more you can do than stand by and watch the carnage unfold. You feel so helpless. But then a young Elanden female grabs your hand. 'Come this way, quickly!' she urges.

You look at the Doctor. What should you do? If you think you should go with the girl, go to 6. If you think you should stay and try to help, go to 104.

3 | 'Help!'

There's no way you're going to get out of this on your own. You have to call for help, even if it means the native with the bow and arrow!

Eventually your cries are answered — a tall, lanky figure in a long coat arrives at the edge of the marsh. It's the Doctor!

'Got that sinking feeling?' he asks cheekily. 'Thought I'd never find you — luckily I'm an expert tracker and I was able to follow your trail. Mind you, I don't fancy following you into the marsh ...'

He pulls down a long vine from the edge of the jungle and throws the end towards you. 'Grab hold and I'll pull you in!'

Go to 50.

4 You've no choice — you have to try and get through the flames. You take a run and then leap — the heat engulfs you for a moment and you can feel the fire everywhere. Suddenly you're on the other side, rolling through the sand.

The Doctor lands besides you. 'You're on fire!' he yells.

Your clothes are smoking and you can feel the flames starting to catch.

'Roll over!' shouts the Doctor. 'Keep rolling over!'

You roll, trying to put the flames out with the sand. The Doctor wraps you in his coat, smothering the fire.

'It's OK, you're out,' he tells you, pulling you to your feet. 'Come on!'

But it may be too late. The dragon is right behind you, ready to roast you again!

If you want to run, go to 99. If you think running might make the dragon angry, go to 67.

5 You run for your life. The Doctor's leading the way, scrambling through the remains of the thorn bushes which have been burnt.

The dragon screams and sheets of flame pass overhead. The heat on your back and neck spurs you to keep running.

The Doctor leads you into the foliage of a nearby jungle. Maybe you can lose yourselves in the undergrowth?

But there is someone else already here, just emerging from the forest: a team of hunters, short, stocky humanoids with golden skin and dark spacesuits covered with weapons of every description. The Doctor quickly introduces himself.

'We are the Ikonis,' responds the group's leader. 'Hunters from the planet Royal Ikon.'

They're hunting the biggest dragon in existence — the Dragon King of Elanden. They couldn't have arrived at a better time — the Dragon King is approaching!

Go to 69.

6 | 'Come! Follow me, or you will die too! The Ikonis will kill you both!' says the girl.

The Elanden are fighting back, using knives and spears and, when necessary, their bare fists. The Ikonis are taken aback by the ferocity of the counter-attack.

'Perhaps we should get out of the firing line at least,' agrees the Doctor as an energy pulse shaves a lock of hair off his spiky fringe. 'Let's go!'

The girl, whose name is Jarla, leads you quickly out of the village. You follow her up a steep embankment, climbing through knotted undergrowth and ferns.

She stops and points further up the hill. 'You must go that way. All the way to the top.'

She's pointing to the summit of a small, craggy mountain rearing out of the jungle. There's smoke curling from the peak.

'It's a volcano,' you say as you realise what it is.

Jarla nods and urges you on. 'Please; get away while you still can.'

'What about you?' asks the Doctor. 'Why don't you come with us?'

'My place is with my people. Yours is not.' And with that, Jarla turns and disappears into the foliage.

'Well,' says the Doctor. 'The only way is up.'

Go to 49.

7 You approach the village together. The Doctor smiles broadly as you walk up to the gates — a pair of trees with long, supple trunks that have been bent and tied together to form an impressive arch.

The people in the village welcome you cordially. The Doctor tells you that travelling in the TARDIS allows you to understand what they are saying. You can hardly believe your luck — a chance to talk to an alien race!

'You are strangers to our world,' says a village elder, 'but you are not our enemy. Come and sit with us, share our food.'

The Elanden are tall, slender people with long, gentle faces. Their big green eyes appraise you carefully but warmly. They wear ornately-patterned animal hides and eat communally around a fire. You can't help wondering who or what could be their 'enemy'.

You enjoy a meal of tasty vegetables and fruit as the Doctor chats with the village elders. Eventually he tells you that you have both been invited into the Gaden's tent.

'Gaden?'

'Their leader. Sort of shaman. Witch doctor, if you like. Don't worry, I'm sure he's more doctor than witch.'

If you go to see the Gaden, go to 33. If you decline the invitation, go to 65.

8 'No, keep quiet,' you urge him. 'We don't know who might hear you — they may not be helpful!'

'True,' the Doctor agrees. He tries again, pulling as hard as he can on the branch. Eventually, by kicking out with your legs as he pulls, you manage to crawl out onto firmer ground. You lie there, cold and wet, and wonder what else this delightful planet has in store for you.

'No time for lying around,' says the Doctor, hauling you to your feet. 'We've got company!'

He's pointing at the ground, and, looking, you see huge centipedes crawling out of the mud towards you. You leap to your feet and find yourself practically surrounded by the giant, squirming insects.

Go to 108.

9 The Ikonis lead you to the fabled Dragon's Graveyard. The journey takes many hours, walking across the marshland, through jungle and eventually down into a deep, misty valley.

The Ikonis tell you that they are hunting for the remains of the greatest dragon that ever lived — a native beast of Elanden believed to have once breathed fire.

'They say the Dragon King burned the ground at his feet with his own breath before he died,' explains the leader, 'in order to purify his final resting place.'

You reach a rocky clearing where the ground is scorched black and a number of huge, curling white bones lie at the centre.

'The Dragon King,' whispers the Ikonis leader reverently.

The Doctor takes a closer look at the body. 'It's quite well preserved,' he remarks.

Go to 86.

10 You head left, climbing through a knotty tangle of vines and creepers which are still swaying. You catch a glimpse of the Doctor's coat-tails disappearing into a narrow gully. Scrambling desperately through the roots and leaves you eventually catch up.

'I think we've lost them,' you tell him, panting.

'Or maybe they just didn't want to follow us,' says the Doctor thoughtfully. You both stop for a breather and you ask the Doctor what he means.

'Maybe there's something in the jungle they're scared of,' he explains.

Whatever the reason, you both know you can't go back. Forwards is the only option. Slowly you press on, clambering awkwardly over twisted, fallen tree trunks, circling venomous-looking snakes and giant scorpions, until you come to some kind of clearing.

In the middle of a huge mound of sand are a number of large, broken eggs. Examining the shells, the Doctor estimates that each one must be roughly the size of a beach ball.

'Whatever hatched out of these is big,' he says.

Could this be what the natives were afraid of?

You may be about to find out, as a loud, ferocious roar fills the air around you.

Go to 14.

11 It's a long, slow climb but it's worth it: the views from halfway up the mountain are incredible. Your gaze roams across the landscape and the Doctor even spots something flying in the distance. 'Look! Could that be a dragon?'

It's difficult to tell. It looks like a bird from this distance.

You carry on up the mountainside, but the going is very tough. It's getting steeper and hotter all the time. You're breathing hard after a while, but the Doctor doesn't seem to notice. He's more interested in the mountain itself.

'Y'know, I think this might be a volcano,' he says.

Eventually you both pause for a rest. You lean against a rock to get your breath back.

'Well?' says the Doctor. 'Do you want to carry on, or go back down?'

If you want to continue to the top, go to 17. If you want to give up and try somewhere else, go to 110.

12 'Hang on!' the Doctor calls down after you. His voice echoes around the rocks. 'I'll go and fetch a rope from the TARDIS!'

He disappears from view and you are left on your own. You've only been on this planet a minute and you're already covered in scratches and bruises.

You carefully climb down the last few rocks until you reach the bottom of a narrow ravine.

And then you meet your first alien.

He's tall, slender, and humanoid — but his skin is a deep blue colour and his eyes shine like green lights. He's dressed in some kind of animal skins and carries a bow. There's a quiver full of barbed arrows at his hip.

If you think he looks friendly and you want to say hello, go to 96. If you don't think he looks friendly and you think you should run, go to 64.

13 | The Doctor brandishes his sonic screwdriver with a grin. 'This should mix things up a bit!'

He activates the screwdriver and as the tip glows bright blue, a shrill scream fills the air.

You stick your fingers in your ears, but you can still hear what the Doctor's yelling:

'Dragons usually have very sensitive hearing — this ultrasonic frequency should send any that are in the area packing!'

You peer out to see what effect the sonic screwdriver has. The dragon you saw is still there, roaring and gnashing its smoking teeth. Suddenly it looks directly at you — and sees the blue light of the screwdriver.

'Uh-oh,' you say. 'Are you sure the sonic screwdriver will scare them off? I think it might be attracting this one!'

If you think the Doctor should switch the sonic screwdriver off, go to 45. If you think he should keep it on, go to 77.

14 It's a dragon — that's the only possible word for it. It's huge and ferocious, with glistening green and red scales and eyes like burning torches. You catch a glimpse of sharp talons and a mouth full of razor-sharp teeth. On either side of its great head are curling tusks.

It lands with a final flick of its membranous wings and then fixes you and the Doctor with a baleful glare. It's like looking into the depths of a furnace. The great mouth opens and a ball of fire erupts from its gullet.

The Doctor pulls you aside, just before the flames incinerate the ground at your feet. You stumble and fall, all too aware that death is only a dragon's breath away.

If you still think you should run, go to 78.
If you think you'd better hide, go to 46.

15 The cave is dark and cold. You stay close to the Doctor as you move inside, every footstep echoing in the blackness.

The cave is long and narrow, and as you explore further, the light of the entrance begins to fade.

The Doctor uses his multi-purpose sonic screwdriver as a torch. Large bugs scuttle away, glowing in the blue light like fireflies. Spiders creep back to the centre of their thick, sticky cobwebs and watch you walk by.

'I thought I felt a breeze just then,' you say. 'Coming from that direction.'

The Doctor points the screwdriver but it's difficult to see anything. 'A breeze suggests another way out of the cave,' he muses. 'Or we can carry on and go further inside. What do you want to do?'

If you suggest to explore deeper into the cave, go to 47. If you decide to try and find another way out, go to 79.

Before you have a chance to move, the gorilla-things grab both you and the Doctor in their huge hands. Ignoring the terrible cries from above, they pull you into the jungle — and away from the TARDIS.

No matter how much you struggle and fight, you can't break free of their grip. The spiky gorillas drag you through the undergrowth.

The Doctor is taking things much more calmly. 'Relax! Enjoy the ride! They may be friendly.'

Somehow you doubt it — they're dragging you towards a jungle clearing, where they throw you down before the most incredible creature you could ever imagine.

It's an enormous, iridescent green brute with row upon row of flashing yellow teeth inside fierce, snarling jaws. Its front paws are armed with lethally curved claws. A pair of menacing red eyes stare down at you.

'Isn't it magnificent?' says the Doctor appreciatively. 'Absolutely beautiful!'

That isn't quite your reaction. You would choose words like terrifying and hideous.

The dragon opens its red mouth wide and tongues of flame flicker inside.

'But,' says the Doctor, 'beautiful and magnificent as it undoubtedly is, I think I would rather admire it from afar.'

If you agree and want to make a run for it, go to 30. If you think it would be safer to try and hide, go to 46.

'We can't go back,' the Doctor says. 'It's not far now — let's give it a go.'

Spurred on by the Doctor's enthusiasm, you continue up the mountain. Your legs are shaking with the strain by the time you near the summit.

'Nearly there!' the Doctor gasps, pulling you up over the last few rocks. The heat is phenomenal; you can feel the sweat running down your face.

'Look at this!' exclaims the Doctor, peering over the lip of the volcano. 'Isn't that worth the climb?'

Inside the volcano is a vast lake of bubbling, red-hot lava. Smoke drifts across the glowing magma, and half immersed in the molten rock, is a dragon.

It's huge, with a magnificent head crowned by vast, curling spines like antlers and narrow cunning eyes.

This is your last chance to go back down the mountain, go to 81. Or if you want to stay and find out what the dragon is doing, go to 43.

18 You run for the jungle. It is difficult to move through, but you are spurred on by fear. You climb over fallen tree trunks and scramble through dangling vines and heavy leaves. An array of animals scurry away from you, disappearing into the purple undergrowth. You know that the deeper you go, the less chance there will be of the Doctor ever finding you. You could stay lost on this planet forever.

You eventually stumble into a clearing. In the middle of it is the most awesome creature you have ever seen. It's the size of two elephants, covered with metallic green scales and flapping a pair of huge wings. Its long, horned head turns to look at you with a pair of shining yellow eyes.

There's only one thing this creature could be — a dragon.

Suddenly the Doctor bursts out of the jungle, waving something in the air to distract the dragon. It's glowing blue and emitting a high-pitched whine.

'Sonic screwdriver!' he explains hurriedly.

The Doctor tells you that he has used the sonic screwdriver to track you down in the jungle, but that there are other dragons approaching. The one in front of you roars and a jet of flame nearly roasts you on the spot.

Go to 99.

19 | The Dragon King allows you both to climb onto his back. It's a nerve-wracking experience. You don't want to make him angry by stepping somewhere you shouldn't!

His giant wings flap and the Dragon King suddenly takes to the air. You and the Doctor cling on to the sharp spines which sprout from the creature's backbone. If you let go, you'll fall off! Soon you are flying over the mountains and jungles of Elanden. The view is breathtaking, though you feel a bit too scared to enjoy it properly.

Eventually, the Dragon King comes in to land. You're pleased to see that even the Doctor looks a bit wobbly on his feet as he climbs down, but the sight of the TARDIS soon settles his nerves.

'That's the most incredible journey I've ever made,' you tell the Dragon King. 'Thank you!'

But the Dragon King shakes his mighty head. 'No — the most incredible journey you have made is the one that brought you here in the first place. Now I suggest you return.'

'He's right,' laughs the Doctor, opening the TARDIS door. 'Come on — there are plenty more incredible journeys to come.'

This is the end of your adventure on this planet.

20 | You immediately turn to leave — only to find yourself surrounded by the strange-looking people. They don't look very friendly, but the Doctor still smiles brightly and says, 'Hello!'

The natives seize you both and tie you up. They carry you back to their village and throw you down in front of the fire. You can see bones sticking out of a big cooking pot and you can guess who's going in there next.

'You don't think they're going to eat us, do you?' you wonder nervously, already trying to loosen your bonds.

'Oh, they won't want to eat me,' the Doctor assures you. 'Not enough meat.'

You wonder if that means you're first for the pot — but then the villagers are distracted by the sound of a loud roaring noise from overhead. You try to peer up into the sky but you can't see much for the smoke.

If you think you can hear a spaceship overhead, go to 60. If you think you can hear some kind of flying animal overhead, go to 92.

'Let's take it for a quick spin!' says the Doctor with a gleam in his eye. 'We can always bring it back again — but at least we'll have the chance to take a good look at the area, and maybe spot the TARDIS.'

He sits in the pilot's chair and powers up the engines. Soon the ship is blasting off, leaving the jungle far below. You watch through the porthole as the ground sweeps past and then something grabs your attention.

'Look, down there!' you say, pointing. 'Just on the edge of that mountain range.'

The Doctor steers the ship towards the nearest hilltop and sets it expertly down. He's already out of his seat and heading for the exit before the engine sound has died.

'I thought I saw a dragon,' you explain as you catch up.

'You did,' says the Doctor sadly. He's staring down at a huge body lying in the dust. You can see green scales and long, twisted wings above a forked tail. 'But I'm afraid it's dead.'

If you stay to examine the corpse, go to 86. If you think you should leave it alone and explore the mountain, go to 54.

It could be dangerous to wander on-board a strange spaceship. You back away quietly and bump straight into someone — the Doctor!

'Shh!' he puts his finger to his lips and drags you back into the jungle.

'How did you find me?' you ask.

'I didn't find you. You found me! I've been watching that spaceship. I'm pretty sure it's from the Ikon planetary system. They're hunters — ruthless and amoral but very efficient.'

'What should we do?' you ask, sensing that the Doctor isn't impressed.

'I want to take a closer look. Come on.'

Go to 73.

The Ikonis invite you aboard their spaceship for talks.

'I wonder why we've been so honoured?' the Doctor ponders quietly as you follow the alien up the ramp into the ship.

The Ikonis leaders explain why they have come to the planet Elanden: they are hunting the largest and fiercest of all the dragons on Elanden. It is part of the Ikonis culture, a right-of-passage for members of the Royal Household to prove their worthiness as potential rulers. It is a mission of courage and honour to kill and eat the Dragon King.

'Using high-energy weapons and hyperdrive spacecraft,' comments the Doctor wryly. 'Hardly even sporting.'

'We do not hunt for sport,' argues the Ikoni leader. 'We hunt for food — the dragon meat makes us strong and noble.'

If you don't approve of hunting the dragons, go to 90. If you don't think you should interfere in an alien tradition, go to 55.

24 | But the Elanden is too badly wounded. Not even the Healing Ground can save him now.

'I'm sorry,' the Doctor says sadly to Jarla. 'It's too late for him.'

'Wait a minute,' you say. 'What's that? Sticking out of his neck?'

There is a tiny thorn embedded in the flesh of the man's throat. The Doctor plucks it out and examines it through his glasses. 'Some sort of poisonous dart!'

The Elanden immediately starts to cough and splutter. He tries to sit up and Jarla helps him.

'It must have acted as some kind of paralysing agent,' the Doctor surmises. 'Good job you spotted it!'

Jarla's father seems to be recovering well, thanking both you and the Doctor profusely.

But the Doctor is already distracted by something else. He wrinkles his long nose and says, 'Can you smell something funny?'

If you think you should leave it and go, turn to 89. If you think you should investigate, go to 59.

25 The Dragon King carries you to a broad, smoking plain of rock at the centre of a volcano. There are many bones scattered around and the carcasses of strange-looking creatures.

Smoke drifts across the eerie nest as the dragon settles down and tosses you to the ground.

'Is this some kind of nest?' you wonder, rubbing your bruised shoulder.

'Undoubtedly,' agrees the Doctor. 'Full of dragon trophies too, by the looks of it.'

The Dragon King stretches and yawns as a puff of flame erupts from his throat.

'Do you think we're trophies or food?' you ask.

'Let's not wait around to find out,' says the Doctor quietly. 'Look over there.'

He nods to the far side of the nesting area, where, through a veil of smoke, you see a familiar blue box.

'The TARDIS!' you gasp, but the Doctor quickly puts a finger to his lips and you realise that now is not the time to attract attention.

'Another of the Dragon King's trophies?' whispers the Doctor.

Go to 72.

26

'I think we'd better leave,' the Doctor whispers.

You creep away as quietly as you can — although there is already a commotion in the nest. You've been spotted!

'Run!' yells the Doctor, and together you sprint into a ravine. Slipping and sliding down the rocks, you end up battered and bruised at the bottom of a narrow gulley.

'I think we've given them the slip,' you say, ruefully, massaging your twisted ankle.

The Doctor says you should rest for a minute. It is very quiet. After a while, the Doctor straightens up and sniffs the air.

'Phew! Can you smell something?' he asks.

Now he mentions it, there is a strange odour in the air — a musty, rank stench drifting along the ravine.

Go to 59.

27 You slam the doors shut. The grinding, roaring noise still fills the air.

'Right,' shouts the man, 'now help me with this! Come on, quick! Allons-y!'

The ground is moving under your feet as you stagger up a metal gangway toward the console. The man is pointing at the flashing green panel on the circular bank of controls. 'Hit that!' he yells. 'With the hammer, preferably!'

You grab the hammer he points at and give the console a hefty whack. The ground was shaking beneath your feet but suddenly everything is still and quiet.

'Brilliant!' the man says, and claps you on the back. 'Sorry about that, bit of an emergency, the adjacent time anchor was slipping. Could've been bad — but you saved the day. And the night, come to think of it. I'm the Doctor, by the way.' His eyes widen and he grins brightly. 'I wonder where we are?'

He darts over to the doors and yanks them open.

'Uh-oh,' the Doctor says.

> **If you run down the gangway to see what's outside, go to 53. If you wait to see what the Doctor does next, go to 102.**

'We'll try the jungle,' you say.

It's hard going because the trees grow thick and twisted. You have to be careful not to tread on any snakes or disturb any other sleeping animals as you climb through the foliage and over huge, gnarled roots. Creepers hang down from the branches high above and alien creatures chatter and growl in the shadows.

You come across a clearing and find a spaceship. It's gleaming silver and highly advanced, but there doesn't seem to be anyone around.

'Shall we have a quick look inside?' wonders the Doctor, opening the hatch with his sonic screwdriver. You can tell he's curious.

It is deserted but in perfect working order. The Doctor is impressed. 'This is a nice ship but it's been abandoned. According to the log, the crew have disappeared. Fancy a quick trip?'

If you think you should let the Doctor fly the spaceship, go to 21. If you think you should leave it where it is and carry on, go to 85.

'OK,' says the Doctor, 'I think it might be best if we just leave now.'

Several Ikonis are aiming their weapons at you, and you both turn to run.

The weapons fire and a sizzling net of green energy closes around you. Both you and the Doctor are completely paralysed.

But all hope is not yet lost — behind the Ikonis, you see the Elanden arrive. And they're armed. With fierce warrior yells, the native villagers descend on the alien hunters.

The Ikonis turn and fight and it's a fierce contest. The force field holding you fades as the Ikonis turn their weapons on the Elanden.

'This way,' you say, pulling at the Doctor's sleeve. You can see a way out of the fight.

'Wait a minute,' he replies.

If you think the Doctor wants to stay, go to 109. If you think he's seen something else, go to 93.

30 The rocks are all jumbled together like the forgotten building blocks of a giant child. Some are broken, with jagged edges and crumbling surfaces. The Doctor scrambles nimbly over the boulders, directing you to safer footing.

Together you climb up the rocks. 'I think there's a mountain on the other side,' the Doctor comments. You barely have the breath to reply.

Something moves in the dark cracks between the boulders. As you climb over a particularly awkward stone, an enormous centipede the size of a crocodile crawls out of the shadows. It nips at you with its pincers, clearly mistaking you for lunch!

'Quick — this way!' orders the Doctor, reaching down and hauling you out of harm's way. The creature snaps at the air where you had been standing only a moment before. 'This place is full of surprises, isn't it?'

'I prefer nice surprises!' you say.

'The rocks finish here,' the Doctor tells you. 'But there's a steep climb ahead.'

Go to 11.

31 'After you,' says the Doctor as he opens the doors.

You step out onto another world. The view is breathtaking. The TARDIS has materialised on the edge of a cliff overlooking a valley full of jungle. The plants are all bright red and purple and the sky is brilliant amber. You can see several moons and many strange and wonderful flying creatures.

'Careful,' urges the Doctor as you walk slowly forward. 'It always pays to look where you're putting your feet on a new planet.'

You look down and realise that you were about to step into a nest of swarming green ants. But when you move to one side, the ground gives way and you start to fall.

With a sharp yell of fear you tumble down the side of the cliff, bouncing off thorny bushes and getting tangled in tree roots.

If you think the Doctor should climb down after you, go to 44. If you think he should go for help, go to 12.

32 | You don't want to offend your hosts, so you walk forward and enter the tent.

It's dark inside and you can't see anything. But you sense that there is someone waiting in the shadows.

'I wondered when you'd arrive,' says a familiar voice.

'Doctor!'

He gets up and steps into the light, looking fresh and alert. He found a different route down from the cliff top where the TARDIS landed, and stumbled across the village. He guessed you'd turn up sooner or later.

'They've made me a guest of honour here,' the Doctor adds, 'hence the nice comfy tent.'

'So what do we do now?'

'Now we have a choice. The Elanden are having a party tonight in my honour — you can't blame them, really — and obviously we're invited. Or we could make our excuses and leave. It's up to you.'

If you want to stay for the party, go to 68. If you want to leave now and carry on exploring, go to 98.

33 | But once inside the Gaden's tent, the young shaman knocks you both to the ground and hurls abuse at you. It seems not all the Elanden are so friendly.

'You are not our enemy,' says the Gaden, 'but you can help in the fight against them. You will be sacrificed to the Dragon King at midnight!'

He posts guards outside the tent and leaves.

'I didn't like the after-dinner speaker much, did you?' asks the Doctor.

You don't fancy being sacrificed at midnight either. 'We've got to get away.'

'Here's something that may help,' says the Doctor.

If he produces the sonic screwdriver, go to 74. If he picks up a sharp piece of flint, go to 106.

'Come on,' says the Doctor. 'Now's our chance!'

He pulls you out of the tent and you set off at a run. The dragon grabs another villager with a horrible roar.

'Shouldn't we stay and help?' you ask.

'Nice idea,' replies the Doctor, 'but those villagers are deliberately goading the dragon.'

It's true. Many of the Elanden are challenging the creature, hurling abuse and jabbing at it with long spears. The dragon is frightening, but you can't help feeling a little sorry for it.

'Why doesn't it fly off?' you ask.

'It's looking for something — us!'

The dragon steps across the village and rears over you. Its mouth opens wide and a sudden gust of flame erupts from its throat, igniting the tents all around you.

If you try to jump through the flames, go to 4. If you try to dodge and run the other way, go to 36.

35 You decide not to chance calling out. You might attract the attention of the man with the bow and arrows — or something worse. All around the marsh you can hear the sounds of distant creatures growling as they prowl through the mists.

If you keep quiet and don't panic you may stand a chance of getting out. Working slowly and carefully you manage to lift one foot out of the slime and crawl to the edge of the quicksand. Then you can climb out.

There's no time to lose. You must find the Doctor somehow.

After a short walk the mists part and you find a spaceship in a clearing. Its sleek silver lines look out of place in such a savage environment, and there doesn't seem to be anybody around.

If you move in for a closer look, go to 84. If you leave it and look elsewhere, go to 22.

36 'This way!' You set off at a run, the Doctor following behind. Dodging beneath the dragon, you manage to reach the far side of the village without being burned alive.

The pair of you sprint out of the gates and head up the mountainside. Looking ahead, you realise that there is smoke pouring from the summit and a number of craggy vents.

'This is a volcano!' you realise. 'Just our luck!'

'Keep going!' the Doctor urges.

Eventually you see that there are two ways you can go.

If you want to continue to the top of the volcano, go to 49. If you want to hide in one of the cave vents, go to 15.

'Sorry — no can do,' the Doctor tells the Ikonis. 'We're not the hunting type. But if you can just drop us off here.'

Before anyone can move, the Doctor points his sonic screwdriver at the ship's hatch and opens it. Wind rushes through the ship causing panic and confusion for the Ikonis, but the Doctor's grabbed you by the hand and now he's leaping right out through the open doorway!

You tumble madly through the air, certain you're going to die — but then something seems to lower you gently to the ground. As your feet land softly you can't help laughing. 'How did that happen?'

'Antigravity belt,' says the Doctor, showing the device strapped around his waist. 'I nicked one from the Ikonis' equipment store on the way in. Thought it might come in useful.'

The Ikonis ship has circled around and is coming in to land not far away. 'They'll be after us in no time,' you say. 'We'd better get moving.'

'The question is,' says the Doctor, 'which way?'

You can either head up the mountain by going to 75. Or you can head down the mountain by going to 43.

38 It sounds preposterous, but you have little choice. Stay here any longer and Jarla's father will die.

'But magic?' you wonder, as you help the Doctor lift the wounded man. 'Can it be possible?'

'Let's find out,' says the Doctor.

Jarla leads you out of the village and up the hill to a flat plateau. Here the grass has been worn away to reveal a strange, sandy bowl some ten metres in diameter.

'This is the Healing Ground,' says Jarla. 'Lay my father down.'

You do as she says. The Doctor sniffs the air and smiles. 'There's quite a pong here, isn't there?'

'The fumes must be inhaled for the cure to work,' Jarla explains.

'Fumes?'

'This is an ancient volcano,' says the Doctor. 'There are various gases seeping up through the ground from subterranean lava. This area must contain hundreds of healing pathogens.'

**If Jarla's father begins to recover, go to 56.
If he doesn't, go to 24.**

'Let's check it out first,' you suggest.

The Doctor smiles and nods. 'Look before you leap, eh? Very wise. Come on!'

Together you creep towards the edge of the jungle for a closer look. The village looks peaceful enough, although there's a rather fierce-looking man in a ceremonial headdress in the centre of the settlement, waving a number of lethal-looking knives over his head. You can hear his strange chants and cries.

'He's talking about some kind of hunt,' says the Doctor. 'Doesn't sound good.'

'Maybe we should go somewhere else and explore,' you say quietly.

'Good idea.'

But as you turn to creep away, you find yourselves surrounded by a group of natives armed with more knives and heavy batons studded with what look like teeth.

Go to 20.

40 'Maybe if we wait here the lava will cool down,' you suggest hopefully.

The Doctor shakes his head. 'We'll either roast or starve before then,' he tells you. 'Or even die from asphyxiation.'

He's right. The fumes are terrible. You cover your mouths and noses but you can't keep the sulphuric smoke out forever. You don't think matters can get much worse — but they do.

With a great flapping of wings, an enormous dragon lands nearby. It has glowing, golden eyes and a skull full of magnificent, crown-like antlers.

Its great head turns towards you. This is without doubt a king among dragons — huge, powerful, savage and terrifying.

But the Dragon King isn't alone. Behind him you can see a squad of humanoids climbing up the mountain. They appear to be hunters clad in heatproof spacesuits.

'Who are they?' you ask.

The Doctor looks grim. 'Ikonis hunters — proud and merciless.'

The Ikonis are coming up the slope, unseen by the dragon.

Could this be your only hope of escape?

Go to 69.

41 The Doctor breaks off a tree branch and holds it out to you. You can just about reach it — he doesn't want to come too close or he might fall into the quicksand himself. You grab hold of the branch and the Doctor tries to pull you out.

But the mud is sucking you down. It's up to your shoulders now. The Doctor isn't strong enough to haul you out single-handed. 'I'm going to have to call for help,' he says.

You're sinking fast but you're worried that if he calls for help it may attract unwelcome attention. But then what could be worse than drowning in this stinking marsh?

If you think the Doctor should try calling for help, go to 70. If you think he should keep quiet and try something else, go to 8.

You're just too late. You whirl around and slam the police box doors shut behind you, but already the chamber is full of a weird wheezing and groaning noise and the man is hanging onto the console. He looks at you and flashes a quirky grin. 'Don't worry! We've just been thrown a bit off course...'

You stagger across to the central plinth and grab onto a metal rail. The whole place is whirling around like a bucket in a sea storm.

'I'm the Doctor!' calls the man over the noise. 'This is the TARDIS. It's a space—time machine and we're already in flight. Sorry!'

The noise quietens and the bright green lights in the central glass column dim.

'We've landed!' declares the Doctor happily. He grabs a long brown coat from a nearby buttress. 'Come on, let's see where we are!'

Scarcely able to believe what's happening, you follow him down the gangway to the doors.

If you go out first, go to 31. If the Doctor goes out first, go to 88.

43 The dragon speaks to you. It doesn't have a voice, but it uses telepathy — you can hear its thoughts.

'I am the Dragon Queen,' she says softly. 'You disturbed me at my birthing pool.'

'So sorry!' says the Doctor cheerfully. 'We took a wrong turn. We'll leave you to it!'

The Dragon Queen doesn't seem angry; she's more amused than anything. It transpires that all female dragons lay their eggs in pools of molten lava to act as incubators. It's a very private moment, however, and you are considered trespassers.

'But you are alien to this world,' the Dragon Queen says, 'and it is full of many dangers. I sense that you are good people, and offer you the chance to leave unharmed.'

You gratefully accept a lift from one of the Queen's minions — a young male dragon which carries you both in his claws, all the way back to the TARDIS. The view as he flies over the land is both magnificent and terrifying.

The dragon leaves you without a word and returns to the volcano.

The Doctor unlocks the TARDIS door. 'Had enough?'

You shake your head. 'Let's try somewhere else — homework can wait.'

Your adventure on this world is over.

44 'Hang on!' the Doctor calls down. 'I'll be there in a mo.'

You cling onto the branches of a thorn tree as he climbs down. Your fingers are cut and bleeding and you're covered in lumps and bruises already.

'Exploring the universe isn't for the faint-hearted,' explains the Doctor as he helps you down over the last few rocks.

You're both standing at the bottom of a narrow ravine. There doesn't seem to be any way out and neither of you fancy the climb back up — at least, not yet. You're on a different planet — with the chance to explore!

'Look,' says the Doctor, pushing past some straggling vines. 'Here's a cave or something.'

Go to 15.

45 'I'll switch it off,' says the Doctor. The whine dies away and the screwdriver stops glowing. For a long moment there is nothing but silence and you wonder if the sonic screwdriver has damaged your hearing.

But no — the dragon's just listening for something else. It looks like switching the noise off has only maddened it! The dragon sucks in a massive lungful of air, throws back its head and then gives vent to a mighty, fiery roar. Flames shoot up into the night sky like a fountain of light.

'Whoops,' says the Doctor as the flames ignite some of the dry tinder and brush around you.

If you think you should make a break for it, go to 4. If you think the Doctor will have a better idea, go to 107.

'Quick, hide,' you say, pulling the Doctor towards a cluster of broken huts. It must be an old, abandoned village. In the middle is what looks like a large, hollow tree trunk lying on the ground. But when you try crawling inside it feels very squishy and there are insects everywhere.

'Ugh,' you say, spotting the remains of a number of large, curved bones. 'What is this?'

'I think you've chosen to hide in the carcass of a dead animal,' the Doctor informs you. 'This is all that's left of its rib cage, by the looks of it. What a pong!'

The stench is horrendous — but it might work in your favour. 'If the dragon hunts by scent, it'll never find us in here,' the Doctor points out.

But the dragon doesn't hunt by scent. It finds you very quickly, staring down into the old cadaver with one glowing eye.

'Run!' yells the Doctor, scrambling out of the other end. You're hot on his heels — and so is the dragon! A blast of fire engulfs the bushes which surround you.

If you think you can jump through the flames, go to 4. If you think you should retreat before you get burned, go to 36.

You go deeper into the cave. It gets colder and darker with every step. The Doctor's sonic screwdriver provides some light, but casts strange-looking shadows on the rocky walls around you. Weird insects, and other creatures you can't describe, scuttle away as the blue light touches them.

Others are attracted by the noise and light.

'We'd better hurry,' says the Doctor as you hear something following you through the cave. 'This way!'

He's found a way out and even though it's a tight squeeze you both manage to crawl into the daylight at last.

Blinking in the glare, you can't quite believe where you are.

Directly in front of you is the TARDIS!

But that's not all. Guarding the police box is a dragon — huge wings twitching and tongues of flame licking from its mouth. And there are more dragons lurking behind it.

If you can sneak past to get to the TARDIS, go to 111. If you think you'd better get out of there before it spots you, go to 26.

The larger dragon immediately attacks. It is a vicious, ugly contest. Teeth snap at exposed throats and all the while, the two beasts scream and howl in rage and pain.

You and the Doctor crouch behind a rock, hoping you won't get caught up in the battle.

Eventually the big dragon is victorious: with a final blast of fire, it pins the other creature to the ground. Then it sinks its hideous fangs deep into the other's throat and bites it clean in two.

The victor turns and looks directly at you and the Doctor. You realise that your hiding place is really quite pathetic. It looks like it could all be over for both of you.

'Sorry about that,' says the dragon softly. 'But it's a dragon-eat-dragon world.'

You can hardly believe it. This ferocious beast sounds so intelligent! Nervously you step out from behind the rock and the Doctor introduces himself.

'I am the Dragon King,' replies the awesome creature. 'This planet isn't safe for the likes of you two.'

'I'm afraid we're a bit lost,' apologises the Doctor. 'Have you seen a small blue box with a light on top anywhere?'

'As a matter of fact I have,' says the Dragon King. He spits out the last few fragments of skin and bone. 'Fancy a lift?'

If you think you should take the offer of a lift, go to 19. If you'd rather carry on up the mountain, go to 17.

49 'We'll carry on up the mountain,' says the Doctor.

It's a hard climb up a steep, rocky slope. There's little in the way of vegetation. The surface underfoot starts to become loose and you have to use both hands and feet. A river of shale clatters down the slope behind you, dislodged by your progress. Dust swirls, obscuring your view of the summit.

'This way,' suggests the Doctor, helping you onto a wide section of hard rock. You stop for a rest, breathing hard. 'It's a lava stream,' the Doctor explains. 'Must have poured from the volcano at some point in the past and cooled down until it became just rock.'

'I'm not sure I can go on,' you gasp. The heat is incredible now and the air is thick with choking fumes.

If you think you should give up and go back down the mountain, go to 81. If you continue climbing, go to 113.

The Doctor rolls up a length of creeper and then throws it to you like a rope. Looping one end around a stout tree trunk, he hauls you slowly to the surface of the quicksand. Soon, lying flat, you are able to crawl onto firmer land.

You lie there, trying to get your breath back, wondering how you're ever going to get dry.

'We should find some shelter,' says the Doctor. 'I thought I saw some caves over in that direction.'

Still dripping, you trudge after him towards the rocks. In between some of the larger boulders is a dark opening. It doesn't look very inviting, but you can hear the cries of many strange beasts gathering in the marshland behind you. Suddenly the cave looks quite promising — but what if you get trapped in there?

If you want to try the cave, go to 15.
If you want to head back to the jungle, go to 28.

51 | 'We'll have to try and outrun it,' snaps the Doctor, pushing you on ahead. You both hurtle down the mountain, and you can feel the roasting heat of the lava behind you. But there is no way you're going to make it all the way down.

'Quick!' you gasp. 'Get behind this!'

You've spotted a large boulder stuck in the mountainside and, with a desperate heave, you throw yourself behind it. The Doctor joins you a moment later, just as the stream of molten lava hits the giant rock. The glowing river is bisected, flowing either side of the boulder and you are safe — for the moment.

If you think you should wait here for the lava to cool, go to 40. If you think you should try calling for help, go to 58.

52 As politely as you can, you decline the invitation. At the very least you suspect a trick — and at best it would be impossible.

But the Dragon King is a proud beast and you can see he's offended. His golden eyes narrow to fierce slits and an ominous rumble builds in his throat, emerging as a ball of fire.

'Whoops,' says the Doctor grimly. 'Now we're for it.'

But all may not be lost — behind the Dragon King you can see Ikonis hunters wearing suits of golden space armour. They are climbing slowly up the hill towards you, weapons drawn.

Go to 69.

53 You run out of the TARDIS after the Doctor. He's already striding to the top of a rocky slope, his long brown coat-tails blowing in the wind.

Hang on. This is just weird. The sky is a deep burgundy colour, lit with pale amber clouds and a number of moons. The ground beneath your feet is composed of gritty, dark green sand.

'This is an alien planet!' you yell, catching up with the Doctor.

'Yeah,' he replies casually. 'It's called Elanden. They say it's a world of outstanding natural beauty, and I can see why.'

He's right. Stretching before you is a fantastic vista of mountains and jungle. The plant life is rich in every shape and colour.

You spot a settlement of some kind in the next valley. Tall, beautiful people move around the simple huts and tents.

'Looks like paradise,' says the Doctor. He turns to you with a quizzical look. 'Shall we introduce ourselves?'

If you think you should introduce yourselves to the villagers, go to 7. If you think you should be a little more cautious, go to 39.

'Let's leave it in peace,' you say. 'We can check out the mountain instead.'

This sounds good to the Doctor, and together you head off to explore the volcano. It's extremely hot and dusty and there is a large cloud of steam creeping from the summit up into the amber sky. Large winged creatures fly around the column of smoke and you wonder if they could be dragons.

'Only one way to find out,' says the Doctor. 'Carry on up to the top and take a closer look.'

'Do you think it's safe?' you ask.

He shrugs. 'Nothing's safe on this planet.'

If you want to carry on up to the top, go to 49. If you would rather head back down the mountain, go to 81.

'Of course we approve,' says the Doctor quickly. At first you can't believe it — the Doctor can't be condoning this kind of ceremonial bloodshed! But then he catches your eye and winks. You become very aware of the fact that you are surrounded by heavily armed and probably hostile aliens.

'Then we will show you the Dragon King,' announces the Ikonis leader eagerly.

'Brilliant,' says the Doctor.

The Ikonis fly their spaceship to the nearby mountain range where the peaks are little more than lava-filled craters. Thick smoke drifts from the volcanoes.

'This is Dragon Mountain,' says the Ikonis pilot, indicating the largest and most active volcano. 'Now you may join us in the hunt!'

If you think you should continue to play along, go to 63. If you think you should decline the offer, go to 37.

The Elanden shows signs of recovery very quickly.

'Thank you so much,' Jarla says, addressing both you and the Doctor. 'Without your help my father would have died.'

'I still don't understand how the Healing Ground works,' you say.

'It belongs to the Dragon King,' the girl explains. 'Look!'

She points into the sky, where a distant, winged shape is fast approaching. Within seconds you can hear the loud sweep of its elegant wings and a giant dragon swoops down to land nearby. It throws back its long, scaly head and roars. Green flames leap from its nostrils.

'Numismaton gas!' exclaims the Doctor in delight. 'It breathes pure numismaton gas — renowned across the universe for its healing properties. Mixed with the volcanic pathogens in this area, no wonder it has such an effect!'

Jarla's father is already thanking you profusely. He explains that the Dragon King is a friend of the Elanden, and they always defend its breeding grounds from alien hunters like the Ikonis.

With a final, long look at the magnificent Dragon King, you head back for the village. The Elanden have fought well and the Ikonis have retreated to their spaceship.

'And I think it's about time we retreated to ours,' says the Doctor. The grateful Elanden escort you both back to the TARDIS, where you make your farewells. Jarla gives you an iridescent dragon feather as a souvenir.

'Enjoy your trip?' asks the Doctor when you're inside the TARDIS. He's already setting the controls for Earth.

You nod and smile broadly. 'Beats homework, any day!'

Your adventure on this planet is over.

You enjoy the sensation of falling through the air — you can see the Doctor, far below you, his coat-tails flapping like wings. It's easy to control the antigravity belt, and soon you catch up with him. Together you fly over the Elanden landscape, past great jungles and mountains, rivers and marshes.

The Doctor calls across to you: 'Look over there! We're not alone!'

It's difficult to hear him over the rush of the wind, but you can see where he's pointing — flying alongside you is a huge, scaly creature with giant bat-like wings and a long, reptilian head. It's a dragon.

But that's not all. The Doctor's gesticulating madly and suddenly you see what he's getting at: clutched in the dragon's giant claws is a familiar-looking blue police box!

Wherever the dragon is taking the TARDIS, you'd better follow!

Eventually it comes to land in a large nest made from a volcanic crater. The whole area is strewn with strange bits of debris.

Carefully you drop to the ground with the Doctor. You don't think the dragon's seen you yet, but it will spot you any moment.

If you want to try sneaking past the dragon to the TARDIS, go to 25. If you think you should both get away while you can, go to 26.

You can't stay here forever, so you take it in turns with the Doctor to call for help.

Finally, your cries are answered — although it wasn't what you expected.

With a great flapping of wings, an enormous dragon lands nearby. It has glowing, golden eyes and a skull full of magnificent, crown-like antlers.

But that's not the end of the surprise. When the dragon opens its mouth, it speaks.

'I am the Dragon King,' it announces grandly. Puffs of smoke emerge with each word. 'You are in great peril if you stay on this world. Climb on my back and I will take you back to your ship.'

It seems like an offer too good to refuse — or does it?

If you take the Dragon King up on his kind offer, go to 19. If you decline, go to 52.

Sniffing the air like a bloodhound, the Doctor's already investigating. He follows the strange smell until you stumble on a decaying corpse hidden in the undergrowth.

'It's huge,' you realise as you examine the carcass. It's the size of two bull elephants, with white bones sticking out of a shimmering green skin. The head of the beast is the size of a small car, covered in thick spines. The jaws are long and full of jagged teeth.

'It's incredible,' breathes the Doctor in awe. 'Look — the remains of giant wings here... a barbed tail here... and scorch marks on the fangs. This is the body of a dragon!'

'It must have looked magnificent when it was alive,' you comment, although secretly you're glad it's not alive right now!

There are more dragon corpses in the surrounding area. 'I think we've stumbled on a dragon graveyard,' says the Doctor. 'Come and look at this one.'

Go to 86.

A small silver spacecraft settles on the ground with a blast of noisy landing jets. A hatch opens on the side and a metallic ramp extends.

The beings that emerge are golden, humanoid creatures in gleaming black space armour. They are carrying futuristic energy weapons.

The leader steps forward. His golden skull is topped by a series of barbed antlers like a crown. 'We are the Ikonis,' he announces smoothly. 'Hunters from the Royal House of Ikon. We seek the Dragon King!'

The village Chieftain steps up, holding an ornate spear in one hand.

If you think there's going to be a fight, go to 87. If you think they are going to talk, go to 23.

'We understand how you feel,' says the Ikonis leader. 'But without our intervention, the Dragon King would slay everyone of the Elanden community here.'

The Elanden arrive, offering food and drink to the Ikonis in gratitude. They are treated like heroes. The Doctor argues that it would still have been better to render the dragon unconscious rather than destroy it, but the Elanden disagree.

'The Dragon King is our deadly enemy. He hunts us, destroys our villages, eats our women and children. The Ikonis are our protectors. The meat from this dragon will feed our people for the winter months ahead.'

The Ikonis, it transpires, also use chemicals from the dead dragon to make vital medicines for their own people. The alien hunters and the peaceful native villagers have enjoyed this arrangement for centuries.

The Elanden take you and the Doctor back to the TARDIS. As a parting gift, the villagers give you one of the Dragon King's fangs.

As the Doctor sets the TARDIS controls for home, you wonder if it might have been safer to have just carried on with your homework!

Your adventure on this planet is over!

62 You start walking across the stinking marsh — it's heavy going, and your feet keep sinking deep into the mud. The Doctor tries to find a safe route through the quagmire, scanning the way ahead with his sonic screwdriver.

But it only takes one false step — and you've wandered off the correct path!

You sink into a patch of quicksand — it sucks you down with terrifying speed! 'Help!' you manage to cry as the cold mud squeezes around your chest.

The Doctor whirls around and sees the trouble you're in. Thinking quickly he looks around for something to throw to you — something you can grab hold of. There are some trees nearby, and long, thin creepers trail across the ground. There are also a number of twisting branches. Which should he choose?

If you want him to throw you a creeper, go to 50. If you want him to throw you a branch, go to 41.

The Ikonis land the spacecraft and arm themselves with heavy disruptor rifles and energy nets. They offer you and the Doctor similar weapons, but, taking the Doctor's lead, you decline.

'No thanks,' says the Doctor, as he refuses another blaster rifle. 'It'll only slow me down.'

'You must be very brave to face the Dragon King unarmed,' remarks the Ikonis leader.

'We'll see.'

You file out of the ship. The mountainside is a blasted wasteland of smouldering volcanic rock. You and the Doctor soon take the opportunity to slip away from the hunting party.

'Look what's over here,' says the Doctor, spotting something lying in a narrow crevice in the rock.

It is the corpse of a huge dragon. It's old, the bones sticking up through the dried out flesh, but it is an amazing sight: vast wings, huge claws and a barbed head are still clearly visible.

If you want to stay to examine the remains, go to 86. If you think you would rather leave it alone and explore the area, go to 54.

64 The alien raises his bow and fits an arrow, aiming it straight at you.

You've no choice but to turn and run. You sprint up the ravine and an arrow flashes past your head. Scrambling through some bushes, you wonder where the Doctor is. He'll never find you now!

The alien native is chasing you. As you emerge from the gully, you see the land splits into thick, purple jungle or deep green marshland. You might be able to hide in the jungle — but it will be difficult to move quickly. If you can get across the marsh safely, the alien might hesitate to follow you.

If you want to try the jungle, go to 18.
If you want to try the marsh, go to 82.

'Actually,' says the Doctor, 'I think we've already outstayed our welcome.'

He nods towards the Gaden's tent, and you turn to see an enormous man emerge with two gleaming knives in each hand. He's staring at you both with murderous intent.

'Looks like they've been fattening us up for the kill,' says the Doctor. 'Let's go.'

At his signal, you break into a sudden run. The crowd of villagers roar in dismay and set off after you. You dodge and duck and manage to break free, although hands are reaching out for you at every turn.

The Doctor grabs you by the collar and drags you suddenly in another direction, causing a multiple pile-up of villagers. He leads you out of the village and you both sprint into the jungle.

You can hear the sounds of pursuit. It's a long run but you must keep on going, leaping fallen tree trunks and tearing through the foliage.

Eventually you stumble across the mouth of a cave, half hidden by creepers and vines.

If you want to hide in the cave, go to 15. If you think you should carry on deeper into the jungle, go to 28.

66 'We should help them,' you say, and the Doctor agrees emphatically.

'Come on!' He runs towards the melee, waving his arms over his head, trying to distract the dragon. His plan works only too well as the beast turns, opens its mouth wide, and emits a stream of fire, aimed at both you and the Doctor.

You stagger back, twisting away from the heat, feeling the hair on the back of your head singe.

The dragon takes a step or two towards the Doctor, but he's already got his sonic screwdriver out. The tip glows bright blue as he sends a stream of sonic pulses at the dragon.

'Works on dogs,' the Doctor says. 'Why not dragons?'

The creature wilts under the ultrasonic bombardment. With a final roar and a belch of flame, the dragon flaps its great wings and takes to the air.

The villagers cheer loudly, proclaiming the Doctor and you as their saviours. There's dancing and music and the village elders invite you to a midnight celebration.

If you're too tired to party, go to 100.
If you feel like dancing, go to 68.

The way ahead is blocked by thorn bushes and the dragon's right behind you, stalking through a cloud of thick, drifting smoke. You tense, waiting for the final blast of fire.

But then a huge and terrible roar fills the air and something appears through the smoke above the dragon. A pair of vast wings flap, blowing the smoke away and you see a second dragon — far larger than the first — descend.

Its heavy head is surmounted by a crest of jagged red spines veined with gold. Its eyes shine like coal. When it roars, you can see row after row of needle-sharp fangs surrounding a glistening, barbed tongue.

And then there is the fire.

Flames pour from the dragon's throat and the first reptile-monster screams in fear.

And, as the smaller beast twists away from the heat, the big dragon spots you...

Go to 5.

68 You think it's about time you enjoyed yourself and decide to stay for the party.

'Great idea!' the Doctor enthuses. 'I love parties! Love 'em! Music, dance, great food — I love all those little sausages on sticks and the ones with pineapple and cheese cubes...'

He's still chatting away when you rejoin the villagers and preparations are quickly made for a huge party. Night has already fallen and a great bonfire is lit at the centre of the village. Drum music begins to throb and soon everyone is up and dancing in the light of the flames.

But perhaps the revelry attracts unwelcome attention.

A spaceship swoops low over the village with a loud roar of its landing thrusters. Several figures descend rapidly from the ship on anti-gravity beams.

The villagers are running scared. The Doctor drags you into a nearby tent, away from the commotion. 'So much for the party!' he mutters.

Go to 2.

The Dragon King roars but the Ikonis show no fear. Stepping forward as a team, the alien hunters level their weapons.

The dragon breathes fire, but their spacesuits protect them. The Ikonis surround the magnificent creature and, raising their right arms, extend their gloved hands in what appears to be a formal salute.

But then golden rays shoot from the fingertips of each hand and engulf the dragon in a shimmering energy field. The Dragon King throws back his crested head and screams, vomiting fire into the sky. The golden rays intensify and the creature writhes in agony.

The Doctor watches in mounting frustration as the dragon collapses. He twitches once and then lies still. He's dead.

'That was completely unnecessary,' the Doctor says angrily. 'You could have set those energy disruptors to stun, not kill.'

The Ikonis stare at him, and they don't look happy.

You agree with the Doctor, but it might not be a good idea to annoy these proud hunters.

Do you alert the Doctor and try to make a run for it? Go to 29. Do you stay put and wait to see what happens? Go to 61.

70 The Doctor calls out for help — and gets it from an unexpected source.

A group of humanoid aliens march out of the mist towards the edge of the marsh. They are golden-skinned with futuristic black spacesuits.

'We are a hunting party from the planet Ikonis,' says the leader. 'What seems to be the trouble?'

'Stuck in the mud,' says the Doctor, indicating you.

One of the Ikonis hunters points a strange, torch-like device at you. A faint blue beam envelops you and you rise out of the bog without difficulty.

'Antigravity beam!' exclaims the Doctor happily. 'I've always wanted one of those.'

'You mean there's actually something your sonic screwdriver can't do?' you ask ruefully as you begin to dry off.

Introductions are made, and the Ikonis leader tells you that he is hunting the Dragon King.

'Sounds great,' the Doctor replies carefully. 'But — hunting?'

'The Dragon King is already dead,' the Ikonis explains sadly. 'We hunt for his grave.'

Go to 9.

71 | You don't wait to hear any more. You dash down the ramp and open the doors, full of excitement.

You run out into an alien world. The ground is hard and gritty, covered with purple scrub and stiff, razor-sharp grass. Before you is the edge of a dense jungle, stretching away to an horizon of volcanoes. Grey smoke drifts from the summits into a deep purple sky.

You barely have time to take all this in before a number of creatures burst through the undergrowth. They look like gorillas — if a gorilla happened to be covered in spines like a porcupine rather than fur.

'Run!' yells the Doctor, whirling around and heading back to the TARDIS. You race after him but it's too late — the creatures have surrounded the TARDIS. They are jabbering madly and beating their chests with thick, spiky arms.

And then the air is filled with a savage and terrible roar from right above your heads.

If you think these creatures will be frightened off by the roars, go to 75. If you think they won't be frightened, go to 16.

You follow the Doctor quickly to the TARDIS and he unlocks the door. Pausing for a moment to take a last look at this savage, alien world, you see the Dragon King looking straight at you. His roars and a ball of fire crackles towards you... just as the TARDIS doors slam shut. The Doctor's pulled you inside the time machine at the very last second.

'Time to go,' he says with a smile.

And with that, the TARDIS dematerialises. You can only imagine the Dragon King's reaction.

Your adventure on the planet of the Dragon King is over.

73 'Look here they come!' says the Doctor, ducking down behind a rock.

A troop of heavily-armed aliens wearing thick, silver armour arrive. The armour is in fact part of their spacesuits — the Ikonis look very advanced.

A giant centipede emerges from its hiding place among the rocks and scuttles across the clearing. Instantly one of the Ikonis hunters points his wrist-mounted laser weapon at the creature and fries it to a crisp.

'Oh, I don't like that at all,' whispers the Doctor.

But you have been discovered — one of the hunters is pointing a scanner device at the rocks where you are standing.

'Show yourself!' orders the Ikonis leader. 'We know where you are hiding!'

The Doctor looks at you. 'Well? We can either give ourselves up now or make a break for it through the rocks.'

If you think it's safer to give yourselves up, go to 23. If you think you should attempt to run away, go to 30.

The Doctor produces a small, futuristic-looking tool. 'Sonic screwdriver,' he explains quietly. 'Multi-purpose. Never leave home without one.'

He makes an adjustment to the instrument and points it at the thick, leathery fabric at the back of the tent. The tip of the screwdriver glows a brilliant blue and a shrill whine fills the air.

'You'd better hurry or they'll hear it,' you warn.

'Almost there,' the Doctor replies. The material is slowly parting under the sonic rays.

It seems to take forever but soon the Doctor has managed to cut a flap in the tent big enough for you both to squeeze through. But already you can hear some kind of commotion outside.

The guards must have heard the sonic screwdriver!

If you scramble through the hole in the back of the tent, go to 2. If you stop and check the entrance first, go to 97.

The gorilla creatures hear the roars and instantly scatter, terrified. As they disappear back into the jungle, you look up and see a dragon circling overhead. It's huge, with vast, bat-like wings covered in metallic green scales. It circles around and opens its mouth to roar again. Flames erupt from its jaws, scorching the top of the TARDIS.

'That way!' yells the Doctor, and you both sprint for the jungle. There may be spiky gorillas in there, but at least the dragon won't be able to find you easily.

You disappear into the undergrowth with the Doctor and peer out at the dragon. It continues to circle the TARDIS. There's no way back now.

'Let's keep moving,' suggests the Doctor. 'We may be able to approach it from another direction.'

You move off through the jungle. It's exhausting work, clambering over huge, twisted roots and under dangling branches, but at least there is no sign of the gorilla-like creatures.

Eventually you emerge into a clearing, and find a village of simple huts and tents.

'Some kind of civilisation at least,' says the Doctor quietly.

If you think you should go into the village, go to 7. If you think you should stay clear and continue exploring, go to 11.

There's no time to run. The nearest creature lunges for the Doctor, pincers snipping at his throat. You launch yourself at the monster, hitting it hard with your shoulder and knocking it sideways. It squirms on the ground, hundreds of curved, bony legs waving in the air.

'Thanks!' gasps the Doctor, helping you up. The monster twists and turns until it's back on its feet. The others are crawling hurriedly towards you.

'Is it always like this?' you ask.

The Doctor nods. 'I'm afraid so, yes.'

But the other monsters are attacking the one that you tackled.

'It's almost as if they're punishing it for being so weak,' comments the Doctor, fascinated. 'Survival of the fittest — at its most competitive!'

The other centipedes have swarmed over the first, biting into it with their sharp mandibles and chewing on its innards. The centipede thrashes around in the sand until it dies.

'Let's get out of here,' you say.

The Doctor holds you steady. 'Wait — this lot have attracted something else: bigger game altogether...'

He points up into the air, where a huge winged beast is descending, talons spread for the kill.

Go to 14.

'No, wait,' the Doctor says. 'It'll work — it's just a matter of finding the right frequency!'

He makes several adjustments to the sonic screwdriver and then tries again. This time the noise is different; a strange, warbling sound halfway between a whistle and a song.

The effect is immediate. The dragon stops what it's doing, stiffens, and then looks carefully around. It almost seems to be hunting for the source of the noise.

The Doctor stands up, holding the sonic screwdriver out in front of him. The weird sound and the glowing blue tip seem to mesmerise the dragon.

'You've calmed it down all right,' you say.

'Better than that!' exclaims the Doctor. 'Watch!'

He moves the screwdriver and the dragon moves with it. It's as if the Doctor can conduct the creature's every movement — the beast never takes its eyes off the device. Working carefully, he leads the dragon away and then pretends to hurl the sonic screwdriver as far as he can into the jungle. 'Fetch!'

Like a playful dog, the dragon tears off after the sonic screwdriver.

'Now's our chance,' the Doctor whispers, pocketing the sonic screwdriver. And while the dragon is busy searching the jungle for the screwdriver, you and the Doctor quickly leave.

It's a long hike back to the TARDIS. Ushering you back inside the old police box, the Doctor can't help smiling. 'At least you've got something to write about now for your homework — "my trip to another planet"!'

Your adventure on this planet is over!

'Run!' yells the Doctor. You sprint after him, clambering over rocks and through deep crevices. You are scratched and bruised but if you slow down the dragon will roast you alive!

It knows where you are — and where you're heading. With a flap of its great wings it cuts off your escape route, hovering over the rocky slope you're busy scrambling up.

'We're cornered!' you gasp.

'Keep going!' orders the Doctor, pointing his sonic screwdriver at the snarling beast. It won't stop it — but the sudden ultrasonic noise disorientates it just long enough for you to scramble past.

The Doctor rolls beneath a flapping wing and you follow him — and there, half hidden in a cloud of dust, is the TARDIS! The Doctor's brought you back to where you started.

The dragon turns with a roar and you feel the heat of its breath.

'Inside, fast!' shouts the Doctor, throwing the TARDIS doors open. You dive into the police box, crashing onto the metal flooring of the console chamber. The Doctor slams the door shut behind him as a blast of fire scorches the back of his coat.

'That was a bit too close for comfort!' he says, running to the console. He dematerialises the TARDIS double-quick, and soon the time machine is tumbling through the Vortex.

'Let's try somewhere else, shall we?' he suggests.

Your adventure on this planet is over!

79 | 'Let's see if we can find a way out of here,' you say. You head in the direction of the breeze, convinced you can feel fresh air on your face.

'Look at this,' says the Doctor, shining his torch at the cave wall. There are marks here — drawings left by primitive inhabitants of the planet, long since dead. They show humanoid figures running in terror from a gigantic beast with huge bat-like wings and a ferocious mouth full of sharp teeth. In some of the pictures, fire can be seen coming out of the mouths.

'Here be dragons,' comments the Doctor. 'I wish I could have seen a real one.'

They look too fierce for you to want to see a real dragon. Moving on, you find what you really want to see right now — daylight.

You climb out through a narrow crack and follow a dusty trail until you come across a familiar sight — a tall blue box with a lamp on top. The TARDIS!

'That's the thing about exploring the universe,' says the Doctor as he opens the door. 'You never know what you're going to see — you might find a dragon, or you might not. The thing to do is keep looking.'

Once inside, he operates the controls and the TARDIS takes off, taking you to new times and places!

Your adventure on this planet is over!

The larger dragon opens its mouth wide and a jet of flame blasts out at the other dragon. With a scream it flees, trailing smoke.

'Now that's what I call bad breath,' remarks the Doctor.

The huge dragon turns its great, crested head towards you.

'Do you think it can understand us?' you ask quietly.

'I certainly hope not.'

There's nowhere you can run now. At the first step you take, you know the great beast will roast you alive.

The dragon reaches out with its two great claws and grabs both you and the Doctor.

Go to 25.

81 'It's too hot up here,' the Doctor says. 'If we stay any longer we'll fry.'

You head back down the mountain, moving carefully so that you don't slip and fall. However, it's not long before the ground beneath you begins to shake.

'I think the volcano's erupting,' you say, glancing fearfully back. You can see glowing red lava spilling over the lip of the volcano, running down towards you.

'Hurry!' yells the Doctor, pulling you down the slope after him.

A river of molten rock pours down towards you. You're not sure you can outrun it. The heat is intense. You'll have to think of something quickly.

If you think you should hide in one of the cave vents, go to 83. If you think you should try to make it to the bottom of the mountain, go to 51.

The jungle will slow you down too much, so you push on into the marshland.

It's pretty slow-going here too. Your feet keep sinking into the smelly mud and you have to watch very carefully where you tread. One wrong move and you could end up sinking!

The native doesn't seem to be following you, which is one good thing. But the marsh is getting softer and softer. Maybe that's why he's left you to it.

Before long, you find that you can't pull your feet out of the mud. You are steadily sinking in the green slime, deeper and deeper.

If you think you should call for help, go to 3. If you think you should keep quiet and struggle on, go to 35.

83 | 'Quickly!' you shout. 'In here!'

You pull the Doctor into one of the cave vents, just as a massive surge of bubbling lava rushes past the mouth. The stench and the heat are terrible, but at least you're both safe — for the time being.

'That was quick thinking,' the Doctor tells you. 'But now what? Do we wait for the lava to cool and then leave? Or should we explore the cave, see if there's another way out?'

He could be testing you. What should you do next?

If you think you should wait, go to 79. If you think you should go deeper into the cave, go to 47.

84 You cautiously approach the spaceship. It looks deserted but you can't be too careful. There's a ramp leading up from the ground into the spaceship and the airlock looks to be open.

You go inside.

It's cool and bright and clinical. At the front of the ship is a wide bridge area housing the pilot's position and a number of control consoles.

A chair swivels around and you come face to face with the Doctor.

'Wondered when you'd turn up,' he says cheerfully.

You're relieved to see him but he's not alone. The owners of the spaceship are here as well: Ikonis — tall, thickset humanoids in golden space armour carrying a variety of advanced energy weapons.

They are here to hunt dragons.

If you think that sounds like a good idea, go to 55. If you don't like the sound of it, go to 90.

'I think we should leave it alone,' you say. 'If we take it without permission then it could be seen as stealing.'

'Quite right,' agrees the Doctor, although he does look a little bit disappointed. 'Come on, then!'

He leads the way out of the spaceship and locks it behind him with the sonic screwdriver. 'I wonder who it belongs to — and what they're doing on this planet?'

You explore the jungle for a little while longer, eventually climbing up a hillside where the vegetation thins out. Soon you find something else of interest:

'A cave!' You point at a dark opening in the hillside.

But the Doctor's found something else. 'And here's a nest of giant eggs...'

If you want to explore the cave, go to 15.
If you want to take a closer look at the eggs, go to 105.

The body is well preserved — you can clearly see the huge wings, long, serpentine tail and massive head. Huge horns curl up from the skull through the remains of glimmering scales. The eye sockets are huge but empty — you can imagine the eyes having been full of savage life and very frightening. But worse still are the teeth — row after row of jagged fangs lining a pair of immense jaws.

'It must have been a beautiful creature,' says the Doctor sadly.

As he squats down for a closer look, green smoke emerges from the dragon's skull and rises up like a phantom in front of him. The mist takes the shape of the dragon's head in life — horned and with glowing eyes.

'Oh, good trick!' says the Doctor. 'Telekinetic projection — that's just brilliant.'

'You are guests on my planet,' says the mist-dragon in a ghostly voice. 'But you are in great danger. Death awaits you everywhere on this world. You must leave at once — or die!'

'He's got a point,' you say, thinking back to the dangers you have faced since stepping out of the TARDIS.

The Doctor stands up. 'That's all very well — but how are we going to get back to the TARDIS? We couldn't leave now, even if we wanted to.'

The mist billows out from the skull in a huge cloud. The smoke drifts across the clearing, glowing green, and a shimmering shape begins to appear inside. When the smoke clears, the TARDIS is standing before you.

'Aw,' says the Doctor, marvelling, 'I thought the telekinetic projection was a good trick — but that's nothing compared to this! Tele-transportation! Incredible!'

'I think we get the hint, too,' you say.

The Doctor agrees and opens the police box doors, allowing you inside. 'Time we were off,' he says, as you take once last look at the alien world around you.

Then the Doctor follows you into the TARDIS and the doors close. With a grinding roar of its strange engines, the time machine fades away, leaving nothing but a swirl of the dragon's breath behind it.

Your adventures on this planet are over!

'Stand aside for your superiors,' orders the Ikonis haughtily.

The Elanden's response is as brutal as it is instant. His spear strikes the Ikonis armour and draws sparks. Immediately the two sides begin a pitched battle — native spears and arrows against energy weapons. It's a surprisingly equal contest and seems like it's a fight to the death.

The Doctor runs back into the Ikonis spaceship. When you catch up with him he's already at the controls and firing up the engines. 'Time we made ourselves scarce,' he says, and the ship blasts off.

You haven't gone far when the engines stop in mid-flight. 'Drat,' the Doctor says. 'They've remote-controlled the power cells!'

'We're going to crash!' you realise fearfully.

The ship's started to go into a dive, but the Doctor's opened a locker with his sonic screwdriver and produced two complicated-looking belts. 'Put this on,' he says quickly, offering you one. 'It's an antigravity belt — sort of a parachute. Now follow me!'

And with that he opens the airlock and dives out into the air.

You dive out after him into freefall.

If you want to follow the Doctor down to the ground, go to 91. If you want to fly around for a while and explore, go to 57.

You step out onto an alien world and straight into trouble.

You just have time to see that the sky is a rich plum colour above a sandy, rock-strewn mountainside before a terrible creature rears up in front of you.

It's like a cross between a centipede and a scorpion — except that it's the size of a crocodile. It towers over you, heavy mandibles clacking as it tries to bite your head off.

'Down!' cries the Doctor, dragging you into the dust as the creature attacks. You both roll away, scrambling to your feet, but there are more of the monsters rising up from their hiding places in the sand. The TARDIS appears to have landed smack in the middle of a nest of the things.

If you want to stay and fight your way out, go to 76. If you think you should run away as fast as you can, go to 108.

'Let's go,' you say. 'It's great here but I'm exhausted. We've saved this man's life — let's call it a day.'

The Doctor looks disappointed, but agrees in the end. 'I suppose I'd better get you back to Earth.'

'I do have homework to finish,' you admit.

'Oh, don't worry about that. The TARDIS can get you home the moment you left.'

You bid farewell to Jarla and her father and start down the mountain. The Doctor advises you to take a good look at your surroundings. 'Not many people get to walk on an alien planet. Are you sure you want to leave now?'

It's tempting to stay a bit longer.

But then the decision is made for you. Stopping to ponder, you find yourself sinking. Your feet have disappeared into a pool of green mud, and your legs are following.

'Help!' you yell. 'Quicksand!'

'It's a marsh!' shouts the Doctor excitedly. 'That's what I could smell!'

Looks like you're going to stay on Elanden a bit longer. Go to 62.

'I don't approve of hunting,' you say. 'You don't need to eat the dragons at all. You're just trying to prove how big and tough you are. It's pointless and stupid.'

You look at the Doctor and he nods. 'Gotta say, I'm in total agreement.'

'But the Dragon King is a formidable enemy,' argue the Ikonis. 'He is not a helpless creature.'

'He is against laser weapons,' you remark. The Doctor gets up to leave and you follow him.

Outside the ship, you breathe a sigh of relief. 'I thought they were going to stop us leaving!'

'They may yet,' murmurs the Doctor.

Standing in front of you are a group of Elanden natives. They look peaceful but they are carrying spears. The Chieftain wants to know what you have been talking about — but there isn't time to explain. No sooner do you walk into the Chieftain's tent than a squad of armed Ikonis emerge from the spaceship behind you.

If you think they want you, go to 29. If you think they want the natives, go to 2.

The antigravity belt is easy to control. Using a dial on the buckle you can control your speed of descent, and if you spread your arms and legs like a skydiver you can just about steer yourself through the air.

You can see the Doctor below, his coat-tails flapping madly like wings. Beyond him is the broad expanse of the planet below — rocks and crags and jungle. In the distance you can see marshland and volcanoes.

The Doctor comes in to land on a small, rocky plateau and seconds later you touch down next to him.

'That was a fantastic ride!' you say, still tingling with the sensation of freefall.

'One way only I'm afraid,' replies the Doctor, removing his belt. 'Now look at this...'

He shows you a crater where the skeletal remains of a dead dragon are lying in the dust. 'I saw this as we were coming down,' he says. 'Thought it was worth investigating. What do you think?'

If you want to examine the dead dragon, go to 86. If you would rather explore the rest of the area, go to 54.

You look up and see what looks like a dragon descending on the village. It's huge and scaly and abominably ferocious. Flapping its great wings, the giant creature lands by the fire and roars. More flames leap from its mouth, incinerating many of the villagers.

'The Dragon King wants vengeance on the Elanden!' you hear the Chieftain cry, just before he is eaten in one gulp by the dragon.

The Doctor points to a nearby tent and you both dive inside. 'How come we can understand what they're saying?' you ask. 'I thought we were on an alien planet.'

'We are. The TARDIS is translating for you. Don't worry about that, just accept it. That's what I do — otherwise I get a terrible headache. Talking of which, how are we going to get out of this?'

If you think you should get out of the tent and run, go to 34. If you think the Doctor should use his sonic screwdriver, go to 13.

'Look, over there,' says the Doctor, pointing. He's spotted a way through, and something beyond — a large patch of ground in a clearing just visible through the edge of the jungle.

Keeping low, you follow the Doctor through the trees towards the clearing.

'I thought so,' he muses quietly, motioning you forward. You draw level and see what he's found: a number of dragons clustered together, wings gently flapping, smoke snorting from their nostrils.

'What are they doing here?' you whisper.

One of the nearest dragons moves slightly and you can see a number of large, multi-coloured eggs beneath it.

'It's a nest,' whispers the Doctor. 'The females are incubating the eggs.'

But you may have stayed too long. More dragons arrive, landing near the clearing, alerting the females. In a moment, you'll be surrounded.

If you think you should get away fast, go to 26. If you think you should keep still and hope they don't notice you, go to 94.

More dragons arrive. It's getting pretty crowded now, but then a number of Ikonis hunters burst out of the jungle and start firing their weapons. The dragons scream and flames erupt everywhere as they try to protect themselves.

The Ikonis have underestimated the dragons. With savage purpose, the reptiles turn on the alien hunters and destroy them utterly.

Using the mayhem as cover, the Doctor leads you away, and you find the Elanden villagers waiting for you in the jungle.

'We knew the Ikonis would perish,' the Elanden chief tells you. 'No one challenges the Dragon King and survives.'

The villagers take you back to the TARDIS. It is a long journey, but you take the time to talk with these beautiful people and accept a gift: a polished dragon's claw necklace.

'It's time you went home,' says the Doctor as you walk into the TARDIS. 'Back to your homework!'

You clutch the dragon claw. 'Can't we go somewhere else first?'

He starts to operate the controls and then smiles. 'Well — just one more trip wouldn't hurt, would it?'

Your adventure on this planet is over!

You run after the Doctor zig-zagging for cover. The villagers are chasing after you, but you manage to reach the edge of the village and disappear into the jungle. Arrows and spears whistle past, shredding leaves and thudding into trees.

But you've managed to get away, although it's hard work keeping up with the Doctor!

'We can't stay in this jungle for long,' pants the Doctor. 'It's slowing us down too much!'

You see a clearing and head for that. Emerging from the forest, you find that there may be an alternative route: directly ahead is a broad escarpment of rocks and boulders. To one side the ground gives way to a steaming marsh.

The Doctor looks at you. 'Well? What do you think?'

If you want to try the rocks, go to 30. If you want to try the marshland, go to 62.

'Hello,' you say.

The native seems to understand; it's as if travelling in the Doctor's TARDIS has allowed you to communicate with anybody.

'I am Hajin,' says the alien. 'Welcome to my world.'

You are on the planet Elanden. The native takes you back to his village — a large cluster of huts and tents held inside a protective ring of thorn bushes. The Elanden people are friendly and offer you food and drink.

The chief of the Elanden beckons you over to his seat by the fire. He points to a tent at the far end of the village and tells you that you must go inside.

If you go into the tent, go to 32. If you would rather not, go to 101.

'Wait a minute,' you say, peering out through the flap at the entrance. The guards are certainly making a fuss, but they don't seem to be interested in you or the Doctor.

Their attention is taken by something else entirely.

'You're not going to believe this,' you say, 'but there's a dragon outside.'

It's huge and ferocious, a long, sinuous reptile with a massive head crested with vicious red spines and a pair of glowing, golden eyes. There are wings on its back, flapping like those of a bat, and in its claws it holds the remains of one of the Elanden.

There is pandemonium in the village. The Elanden are screaming and running for cover.

The Doctor looks out and grins. 'Wow! A dragon! Brilliant! Isn't it a beauty?'

Beautiful is not the first word that springs to mind. Terrifying is.

If you take your chance and make a run for it, go to 34. If you think you should stay and try to help the villagers, go to 66.

You like the idea of a party, but you're keen to explore the planet. Maybe you can call back later for the festivities.

You make your excuses and leave with the Doctor. The Elanden wave you off as you head out of the camp. But at the gates you are stopped by the Chieftain.

'Beware of the dragons,' he tells you. 'They are everywhere. But most of all, beware of the Dragon King — the biggest and fiercest beast on Elanden.'

It's a fair warning, but you haven't seen any sign of dragons yet.

After an hour's walk you see that the terrain is changing. The Doctor says there's a choice to be made regarding the way ahead.

If you want to head for the mountains, go to 11. If you want to try the jungle, go to 28.

| 'Run!'

You quickly realise that life with the Doctor involves a lot of running.

Flames roar all around you but somehow you manage to break out and head for the jungle. Scrambling through the bushes you eventually find yourselves clambering up the side of a steep mountain. Unfortunately, the dragon has taken to the air and followed you above the trees. It swoops down with a fiery snarl, wings flapping. You're trapped on the mountain.

But then another dragon arrives — much larger, with massive, curled spines growing from its skull like a crown. Its eyes blaze madly and it lunges straight for the smaller dragon.

If you think the dragons are going to fight, go to 48. If you think they'll both turn on you instead, go to 80.

100 You're exhausted. You decline the invitation and retire to one of the tents, where you can collapse gratefully onto a pile of warm furs.

You sleep soundly, only dimly aware of the party going on outside. Eventually you feel someone shaking you awake. It's the Doctor.

'Come and have a look at this,' he whispers.

Outside, the party is over. Across the village, the Elanden lie snoring on the floor and in their tents. All is peaceful.

The Doctor points up at the night sky. Against the stars, you can see something silvery passing overhead with an ominous rumble.

'Spaceship,' explains the Doctor. He looks serious. 'If I'm not mistaken, that's an Ikonis hunting cruiser. This could mean trouble.'

Go to 60.

The villagers seem friendly, but you're not sure about this. 'I'd rather not,' you reply.

'And quite right too,' says a familiar voice from behind you.

It's the Doctor! He's been in the village all the time. He's stepped out of one of the nearby tents with a friendly wave.

'You really don't want to go in there,' the Doctor continues, nodding unhappily at the hut. 'That's where they keep the ferocious fanghog. Nasty brute — loves children. Especially at meal times...'

The Doctor grabs you by the elbow and steers you towards the village exit. 'In fact I think we've both outstayed our welcome!' He's marching you at an increasing speed until you have to break into a run. The villagers are chasing angrily after you.

Go to 95.

The Doctor slams the doors shut and puts his back against them to keep them closed. 'This is a time and spaceship, by the way — and we're in the wrong place and time!'

'What is it?' you ask.

'A platoon of Roman Legionnaires on the march,' he says. 'They're not happy to find a police box in the middle of their battle. Let's go!'

He dashes to the console and flicks some switches. The central column glows as the TARDIS takes off once more — and you wonder what the Roman soldiers thought of that!

The Doctor circles the console, resetting the coordinates. 'Here we go,' he says happily as the groan of materialisation fills the air once more. 'The planet Elanden, in the Andromeda Galaxy. Nice spot, pleasant people, just the ticket.'

'Anything but homework,' you tell him.

He smiles and nods at the doors. 'There's a new world out there. Shall we?'

If you run straight out to see what it's like, go to 71. If you want to the Doctor to go first, go to 103.

The Doctor pulls on his coat and leads the way out of the TARDIS.

You're on a different planet all right: a purple sky stretched over a green desert covered in patches of jungle. Mountains rear up into the clouds, some of them smoking like volcanoes.

'Take a look at these,' says the Doctor after you've explored the area.

He's found a pile of bones stretched out across the gritty sand. Decayed, scaly skin is stretched over some of the bones and the skull is huge, heavy and covered with spiny growths.

'Some kind of dinosaur?' you suggest.

'Dragon, more like,' says the Doctor. He points to an array of slender bones fanning out from the main skeleton, laced with a membrane of dry skin. 'It's got wings.'

'I didn't think dragons really existed,' you say.

'Not on Earth, they don't.' The Doctor stands up, dusting his hands. 'But this isn't Earth.'

If you want to examine the dragon remains more closely, go to 112. If you want to explore the planet a little further, go to 11.

You can't just leave. You look at the Doctor and he agrees without having to say a word.

'You are mad, both of you,' declares the girl in wonder.

'There are injured people here,' you tell her. 'We have to help them.'

Together, you pull a number of wounded Elanden out of the fight. The Doctor says they are suffering from burns caused by heavy-duty disrupter beams.

Crouching down beneath ferocious exchanges of blade and beam, you help several of the wounded from both sides. Eventually you find an Elanden who is mortally wounded.

'This is my father,' cries the girl. 'He will die!'

'Isn't there anything we can do?' you ask the Doctor.

He shakes his head, but the girl, Jarla, has an idea.

'You must take him to the Healing Ground,' she says. 'The air has magical properties there — it is his only hope.'

Go to 38.

105 In the middle of a huge mound of sand are a number of large, broken eggs. Examining the shells, the Doctor estimates that each one must be roughly the size of a beach ball.

'Whatever hatched out of these is big,' he says.

Could this be what the natives were afraid of?

You may be about to find out, as a loud, ferocious roar fills the air around you.

Go to 14.

The Doctor has found a sharp piece of flint lying on the floor. He uses it to cut a slit in the back of the tent and together you crawl out, taking care not to make a sound.

There is a deathly hush in the village. A single mistake now will alert everyone. Centimetre by centimetre, you creep away from the tent. You can see the edge of the settlement just a few metres away.

'At some point they'll see us,' whispers the Doctor. 'We'll have to make a break for it then. Ready?'

You nod. You can't speak because your mouth is dry with fear. Your heart is pounding in your chest, surely loud enough for the natives to hear.

'Now!' hisses the Doctor, and he sprints for the jungle.

You look back when you hear shouts and cries from behind. Your escape bid has been noticed.

But when you turn to leave, you find the Doctor's disappeared into the undergrowth!

If you look for him by turning to the right once your reach the jungle, go to 95. If you look for him by heading left, go to 10.

'This way!' cries the Doctor, dashing off in an unexpected direction. You race after him, well aware of the signs of pursuit behind you.

The Doctor's coat-tails disappear over the edge of a small rise and you leap after him. Next moment you are both tumbling down a rocky incline, throwing up a huge cloud of dust.

'That should keep 'em off our track,' says the Doctor happily. He helps you to your feet at the bottom of the ravine. There are huge rocks and boulders scattered all around you.

'Where are we?'

'Nearly home,' the Doctor announces mysteriously, and you wonder what he could mean — until you follow him around the jumble of rocks and find a familiar-looking police box waiting for you.

'The TARDIS!'

The Doctor unlocks the doors and ushers you inside. 'Hurry up — we don't want any other passengers!'

You both rush inside and he slams the doors shut just before your pursuers arrive. Imagine what they think when the TARDIS dematerialises right in front of their eyes!

'See,' the Doctor says as he operates the controls, 'just like I said — nearly home...!'

This adventure is over and you're heading for home — or are you?

You run, following the Doctor through the nest of writhing centipedes, until you reach the far side. One of the beasts nips at your foot and trips you and the Doctor pulls you to your feet.

'This way!' he yells, heading down the side of a deep gulley. Sand and loose rocks tumble down around you as you stagger towards the bottom of the ravine. You can hear the centipedes scuttling after you.

At the bottom of the mountain slope you stumble into a group of natives armed with primitive weapons. They are blue-skinned humanoids with softly glowing eyes. Behind them is a large village made up of huts and tents and many more people. You can smell cooking.

If you think you should introduce yourselves, go to 7. If you think you should turn and run, go to 20.

'We can't stay,' you tell him. 'It's too dangerous.'

But the Doctor's spotted someone in trouble. One of the native Elanden — a young girl — is kneeling by a fallen man.

'My father is injured!' she cries. 'Please — someone — help us!'

You both run to help, ducking past flashing blades and energy beams.

'He's been hit by a disruptor ray,' says the Doctor, quickly examining the man. 'His chances aren't good — but there must be something we can do...'

'I have an idea,' says the girl, wiping away her tears. She says her name is Jarla.

'Tell me, quickly,' orders the Doctor.

'We can take him to the Healing Ground,' she says. 'The air has magical properties there — it may be his only hope.'

Go to 38.

You agree to try somewhere else and head back down the mountain. You have to move carefully so that you don't slip and fall. At one point you lose your footing on a loose rock, grabbing at the Doctor for support. You both collapse, rolling down the slope in a cloud of choking dust.

There is a sudden rock fall and a chasm opens up beneath you, exposing a boiling froth of glowing lava. The Doctor grabs you and pulls you clear, but the landslide has caused the lava to boil over.

'Hurry!' yells the Doctor, pulling you down the slope after him.

A river of molten rock pours towards you. The heat is intense. You're not sure you can outrun it.

Go to 51.

111 It's a wonderful and terrifying creature – something from a fantasy or a nightmare, you can't decide which.

The dragon rises up, flexing its huge, muscular wings. They block out the sunlight and throw you into shadow.

'It's like a bird of prey,' comments the Doctor quietly. 'Protecting its prey with its mantle.'

'Not the most comforting thought!' you remark.

The Doctor steps forward and clears his throat. 'Excuse me?'

At first you think he must be completely crazy. But the dragon looks at the Doctor with an expression of mild astonishment on its scaly face and says, in a clear, deep voice, 'Yes? What is it?'

'I can't help thinking,' says the Doctor, speaking in amicable tones, 'that a creature as magnificent as you clearly are must also be highly intelligent.'

The dragon thinks about this. 'Well, yes, I suppose so,' it replies, flattered.

'In which case, would I be right in thinking that you would never knowingly eat another intelligent life form?'

'I hadn't really thought about it,' says the dragon. 'I'm the only intelligent being on this planet. When I'm hungry, I eat. And you look like food to me – and far too small and skinny to be intelligent.'

'Good point,' says the Doctor. 'But wrong.'

'Prove it,' says the dragon, licking its lips. Puffs of smoke are curling from its nostrils in anticipation.

'I will — but you'll have to look at that first,' says the Doctor, pointing to the right.

The dragon looks — and the Doctor quickly pulls you to the left, heading for the TARDIS.

Go to 72.

'**A**nd nor is it Elanden,' the Doctor realises thoughtfully. 'The TARDIS is lost. I think this is the planet Haxokros — otherwise known as the Dragon's Graveyard.'

'That doesn't sound very nice!'

The Doctor shakes his head, moving further away to explore. 'It's not. When a dragon dies anywhere in the cosmos, its remains are transported here to rest. No one knows how. No one has ever found Haxokros.'

'Except us,' you say.

'Yeah,' says the Doctor nodding. A grin suddenly ignites his face. 'Isn't that great? Let's explore!'

The Doctor leads you through a crevice which opens out into a vast valley full of bones. The skeletons are huge — and every one of them is the last remains of a dragon. Every different kind can be seen — dragons with wings, with horns, with long, snaky bodies; some which walked on two legs, some with more legs than a centipede.

'It's incredible,' you gasp.

'I've always wondered how the dragons get to be here,' muses the Doctor. "Must be some sort of tele-transportation power in their DNA — kicks in automatically when they die. Sad, really.'

'I think it's fantastic,' you say. 'Look at this!'

You've found the skull of an enormous dragon. It's the size of a small lorry.

'I think you've found the last Dragon King,' says the Doctor.

Go to 86.

113 'Come on,' the Doctor urges. 'Best foot forward. It's not every day you can climb a volcano on another planet. It's not far now — let's give it a go.'

Spurred on by the Doctor's enthusiasm, you continue up the mountain. Your legs are shaking with the strain by the time you near the summit.

'Nearly there!' the Doctor gasps, pulling you up over the last few rocks. The heat is phenomenal; you can feel the sweat running down your face.

'Look at this!' exclaims the Doctor, peering over the lip of the volcano. 'Isn't that worth the climb?'

Inside the volcano is a vast lake of bubbling, red hot lava. Smoke drifts across the glowing magma, and you have to admit, it's an impressive view.

Go to 81.

Step into a world of wonder and mystery with Sarah Jane and her gang in:

1. Invasion of the Bane
2. Revenge of the Slitheen
3. Eye of the Gorgon
4. Warriors of the Kudlak

And don't miss these other exciting adventures with the Doctor!

1. The Spaceship Graveyard
2. Alien Arena
3. The Time Crocodile
4. The Corinthian Project
5. The Crystal Snare
6. War of the Robots
7. Dark Planet
8. The Haunted Wagon Train
9. Lost Luggage
10. Second Skin
11. The Dragon King
12. The Horror of Howling Hill